WALT DISNEY PRODUCTIONS

The

presents

Magic Grinder

Random House  **New York**

Library of Congress Cataloging in Publication Data
Main entry under title: Walt Disney Productions presents The magic grinder (Disney's wonderful world of reading, ≠34) Lord Gurr is taught a lesson about greed when he takes Minnie's magic grinder. [1. Fairy tales] I. Disney (Walt) Productions. II. Title: The magic grinder. PZ8.W1865 [E] 75-11995 ISBN 0-394-82575-6 ISBN 0-394-92575-0 (lib. bdg.)
Manufactured in the United States of America   1 2 3 4 5 6 7 8 9 0

BOOK CLUB EDITION

H I J K
1
R

Once there was a poor maid named Minnie.
She worked for the greedy Lord Gurr.
While he sat in the shade all day, Minnie
and her nephews worked in his garden.
Minnie picked fruit and vegetables.
Morty and Ferdie pulled and cut weeds.

At the end of each day, they brought
their basket of food to Lord Gurr.
He put the heavy basket on the scale.
"Not bad," he would say.

But whenever Minnie
asked for her pay,
he always shouted,
"Come back tomorrow!"
So Minnie had
no money.

Without money, she
could not buy food
for her nephews.

One day she went
to the cupboard.
It was empty.

"I will go and ask
Lord Gurr for some
food," she said.

Minnie went straight to Lord Gurr's house.
He came to the door himself.
"What do you want?" he shouted.
"I am a very busy man."

Minnie peeked into his dining room.
When she saw the delicious food,
she was hungrier than ever.
"I only want a little food," she said.
"My nephews are very hungry."

"Food?" cried Lord Gurr. "I don't have
enough for myself. Go away!"

Poor Minnie.
Away she went
without food for
her nephews.

On her way home, Minnie had to pass a cave.
Suddenly she heard a strange moaning
and groaning.

It was coming from inside.

"I wonder what is wrong?" she thought.

When she stepped into the cave
she was too scared to move.

For on the floor, moaning and groaning,
was a very GIGANTIC DRAGON.

Part of the cave had fallen on him.

"Do not be afraid of me,"
said the dragon kindly.
"I'm stuck under these big rocks.
I need your help."

Minnie was no longer afraid.
"What can I do?" she cried.
"These rocks are too heavy for me."

The dragon pointed to a shelf in the corner.
It was filled with beautiful treasures.
"Take down the golden grinder and bring it
here to me," he said.

Minnie handed the grinder to him.
"Watch and listen," said the dragon.

He began to turn the handle.
As he turned he said,
"*Golden grinder, help me,
please. You will know
just what I need.*"

As soon as he said those magic words,
a shovel was standing beside him.
All by itself
it began to dig.
It lifted
the heavy rocks.

Suddenly another
shovel appeared.
It started
digging, too.

Then came
another shovel,
and another, and
another!

The dragon said,
"*Golden grinder,
stop and stay.*"
The grinder stopped
making shovels.

At last the dragon was free again.

"Because you have helped me," he said, "I'm going to give you this magic grinder. Just say the magic words and it will give you anything you want."

"Oh, thank you!" cried Minnie.

The dragon waved good-by to Minnie.
"Now don't forget the magic words to make
the grinder stop!" he called. "It will not
stop unless you say those very words!"

"I won't forget them," said Minnie.

Away she ran
to show her nephews
the wonderful magic grinder.

When her nephews
saw the grinder, they
were not very happy.

"Where is our food,
Aunt Minnie?"
they cried.

"We will have food,"
she said. "Listen."

Minnie began to turn the handle.
"Golden grinder, help us,
please," she said. *"You will*
know just what we need."

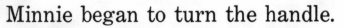

Suddenly the table was covered with food.
There was turkey and ham . . . mashed
potatoes, peas and carrots . . . fruit
and cheese and milk and bread.

Then Minnie said, *"Golden grinder,
stop and stay."*
The grinder stopped making food.

"Oh, Aunty!" cried Morty.
"Let's ask for new clothes."
Minnie said the magic words.

Presto! They were dressed
in fine new clothes.

"Let's ask for new furniture!"
cried Ferdie.

When Minnie turned
the handle and said
the magic words,
the grinder gave them
fine new furniture.

"We are rich," cried Morty and Ferdie.
They bounced up and down on their new bed.

"Just remember,"
said Minnie.
"Never tell anyone
the magic words."

The next morning Minnie and her nephews
did not go to work in Lord Gurr's garden.
Minnie stayed home to plant some flowers.

Morty and Ferdie went fishing at the stream.

Lord Gurr soon came to see why Minnie and
her nephews had not come to work for him.

He was surprised to see their new things.

"All of this cannot be yours!" he cried.

"Where did you get everything?"

"It's a secret," said Minnie.
"I cannot tell you."
"If you don't tell me I'll call
the sheriff," shouted Lord Gurr.
"He will throw you into jail for stealing!"

Minnie showed the grinder to him.

"I did not steal anything," she said.

"This grinder gives me whatever I want."

Lord Gurr snatched it away from her.

"I'll take care of it for you," he said.

And he ran straight home.

He could hardly wait
to try the grinder.
He put it down and
turned the handle.
"I want some
ice cream," he said.

Nothing happened.
"I WANT SOME
ICE CREAM!" he shouted.
Still, nothing happened.

"I will find out how
to make it obey me,"
said Lord Gurr.
Off he ran to find
Minnie's nephews.

Lord Gurr found Morty and Ferdie
fishing at the stream.

"My dear fellows," he said. "I hear you have
a grinder that gives you anything you want.
Tell me—how does this magic grinder work?"

"It's easy," said Morty. "You just say,
Golden grinder, help me, please.
You will know just what I need.
And out comes whatever you want!"

Ferdie quickly poked his brother.
"That's a secret!" he whispered.
Morty did not say another word.

"Very interesting," said Lord Gurr.
And he ran back to his house.

Now he knew how to make the grinder work.

He began to turn the handle.

In his greediest voice he said,

"Golden grinder, help me, please.
You will know just what I need."

Sure enough—the grinder began to make
ice cream!

Then it made more ice cream.
"Stop!" cried Lord Gurr.
But he did not know
the magic words.
So the grinder did not stop.

It made Popsicles, sundaes,
and ice cream cones.
It made chocolate,
and strawberry,
and peppermint.

Soon Lord Gurr had no more bowls
to hold the ice cream.

Ice cream began to spill onto
the floor.

Still, the grinder did not stop.

"STOP!" screamed Lord Gurr, for he was
up to his ears in ice cream. "I'm fre-e-e-zing!"
But the grinder kept making ice cream.

Lord Gurr grabbed the grinder and
began to run.

He ran all the way to Minnie's house,
leaving a trail of ice cream behind him.

When he reached her house, Minnie
met him at the door.

He threw the golden grinder at her.

"If you will just make it stop," he cried,
"I will never bother you again!"

"Oh, my," said Minnie with a smile.
"It *is* making quite a mess. *Golden grinder,
stop and stay*," she whispered.

The grinder stopped making ice cream.

When he got home, Lord Gurr had
quite a job cleaning up all that ice cream.
It took him a whole week.

As for Minnie and her nephews—
they never went to work for Lord Gurr again.
Minnie sewed in her own shady garden.

Morty and Ferdie spent their time fishing.
And the magic grinder gave them everything
they needed to live happily ever after.